It was a rainy day, too wet to go outside. Mummy said,
"Let's make cupcakes! What colour do you want?"

"Pink!" I said. "Pink, pink, pink!"

Mummy put in some pink.
"More!" I cried.
"More, more, more!"

WRITTEN BY Victoria Kann & Elizabeth Kann

ILLUSTRATED BY Victoria Kann

h
Hodder
Children's
Books

A division of Hachette Children's Books

To Jaison and Ashley
E.K.

To Christina and Leigha
V.K.

And to our parents, Patricia and Steve,
with a special thank you to Jill.

CUPCAKES FOR ALL!

Pinkalicious

First published in the US in 2006 by HarperCollins Children's Books. First published in the UK in 2015 by Hodder Children's Books.
Text copyright © 2006 by Elizabeth Kann and Victoria Kann
Illustrations copyright © 2006 by Victoria Kann
Pinkalicious and all related logos and characters are trademarks of Victoria Kann, used with her permission.

Hodder Children's Books, 338 Euston Road, London, NW1 3BH
Hodder Children's Books Australia, Level 17/ 207 Kent Street, Sydney, NSW 2000

The right of Elizabeth and Victoria Kann to be identified as the authors and Victoria Kann as the illustrator of this Work
has been asserted by them in accordance with Copyright, Designs and Patents Act 1988.

A catalogue record of this book is available from the British Library.

ISBN: 978 1 444 92161 8
10 9 8 7 6 5 4 3 2 1

Printed in China

Hodder Children's Books is a division of Hachette Children's Books. An Hachette UK Company.

www.hachette.co.uk
www.thinkpinkalicious.com
www.facebook.com/pinkalicious

I gobbled up a couple of cupcakes while Mummy and I iced them. They were so yummy – they were PINKALICIOUS!

I offered one to Peter, my little brother, but he is very picky and didn't want to eat his. So I ate it.

"Please, Mummy, can I have JUST ONE MORE?"
I begged when I woke up from my nap.

"You get what you get, and you
don't get upset," she said.

But I got **very** upset.

After dinner I ate more
cupcakes. Then I refused
to go to bed. "Just one more
pink cupcake, and I'll go
to sleep," I promised.

Daddy waved a
tired finger at me.
"You have had ENOUGH!"

The next morning when I woke up, I was PINK!
My face was pink, my hands were pink,
and my tummy was the colour of a sunset!

Daddy thought I had played with
markers, so he gave me a bath.
The pink did not come off.

I cried because I was so beautiful. I even
had PINK tears. I put on my pink fairy
princess dress and twirled in front
of the mirror, while Mummy
speed-dialled the doctor.

"I'm Pinkerbelle! Look at me,
I'm Pinkerbelle!" I sang.
"Just one more cupcake!
PLEASE JUST
ONE MORE!"
I yelled on the way
out of the door.

Mummy took
me right to the
doctor's office.

Doctor Wink looked at me and said,
"You have a very rare
and acute case
of Pinkititis."

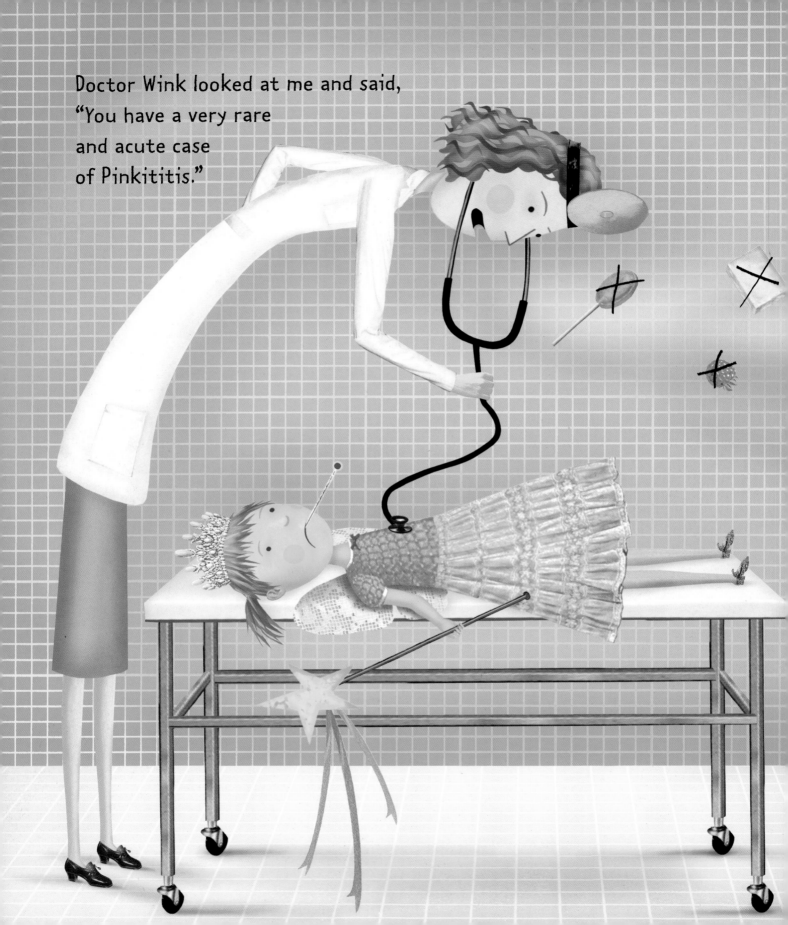

I guess that's not the worst thing that could happen.
Just call me PINKERELLA!

Then Doctor Wink said, "For the next week, no more pink cupcakes,
pink bubble gum or pink candyfloss." (BOO!)
"To return to normal, you must eat a steady
diet of green food." (YUCK!)

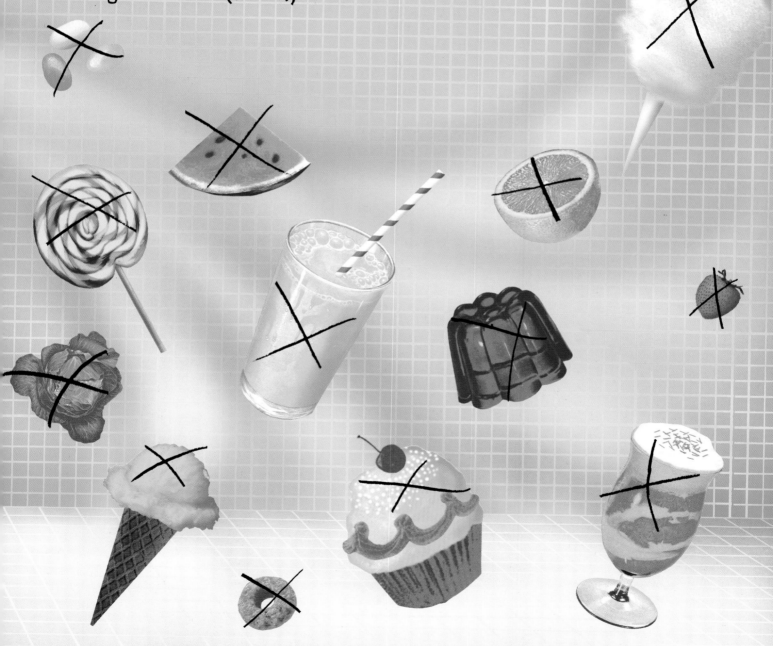

On the way home, we stopped at the playground. My friend Alison was there, but she didn't see me because I blended in with the pink peonies.

When I waved to Alison, a bumblebee landed on my nose. **"Buzz off! I am not a flower!"** I scolded the bee.

Soon I was surrounded by bees, butterflies and birds.
"MUMMY," I cried, "please take me home!"

When we left the playground, I asked Mummy if I could eat another pink cupcake when we got home. "Don't you remember what the doctor told you?" she said. "NO MORE CUPCAKES!"

Peter tugged at my pinktails. "I wish I were pink like you," he said. He was green with envy.

That night, I pretended to eat my dinner
of mushy, dark green vegetables.
After everyone went to sleep,
I sneaked into the kitchen, climbed
onto a chair, and reached on my
tippy-toes to the top of the
fridge, where Mummy
had hidden the cupcakes.

I
took just
one
more
pink
cupcake
and ate it.
Then I
licked
the
pink
cupcake
wrapper
clean.

When I woke up in the morning, I felt different.
I ran to the mirror and peered at my reflection.
I was a deeper pink than I had ever seen. In fact,
I was no longer pink.

I WAS RED!

"Oh, no, not red!" I screamed.
I didn't want to be red. I should NOT have eaten that pink
cupcake last night! I wanted to be myself again.
I knew what I had to do...

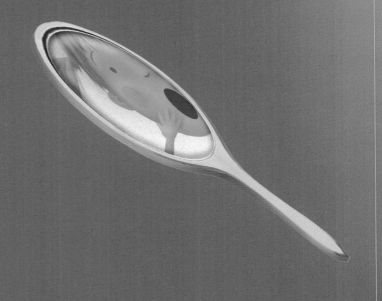

I opened the fridge, held my nose,
and squeezed a bottle of icky green
relish onto my tongue. I ate pickles
and spinach and olives. I swallowed
artichokes, grapes and Brussels sprouts.
Next thing I knew, my arms tickled,
my ears tingled and my feet twitched.

Green Tea

RELISH

SUGAR PEAS
HONEY POD

I was no longer red. I was no longer pink.
I was me, and I was beautiful.

"So what happened to the rest of the
cupcakes, Pinkalicious?" Daddy asked.

Just then Peter ran in and yelled...

"PINK-A-BOO!"